This
MOUSE ⬚ WORKS
Classics Collection Storybook

belongs to

Kayla and Magnard

DISNEY'S
THE HUNCHBACK OF NOTRE DAME

MOUSE
WORKS

© 1996 The Walt Disney Company
Printed in the United States of America
ISBN: 1-57082-173-9
1 3 5 7 9 10 8 6 4 2

One morning, as the bells of the great Cathedral of Notre Dame echoed over the rooftops of Paris, a gypsy performer named Clopin entertained a crowd of eager children gathered before his puppet theater.

3

"Listen," said Clopin, "they are beautiful, no? But, you know, the bells do not ring themselves."

"They don't?" asked the puppet Clopin wore on his hand.

"No," answered Clopin, pointing to the bell tower. "Hush, and I will tell you the tale — a tale of a man . . . and a monster."

8

The children listened as Clopin told the
story of a gypsy family who, nearly twenty
years before, had slipped into Paris only to
be met at the dock by the evil Judge Claude
Frollo and his brutal soldiers. Frollo despised
gypsies, for to him they represented all that
was bad in the world.

As the family was taken prisoner, Frollo noticed the gypsy woman clutching a bundle. He commanded the soldiers to seize what he thought were stolen goods. The terrified woman ran across the square, then up the steps of the magnificent Cathedral of Notre Dame. Desperately, she pounded on the doors crying, "Sanctuary! Please give us sanctuary!"

Frollo thundered up behind the woman on his horse and grabbed the bundle. They struggled, and she fell upon the stone steps and struck her head. As Frollo looked upon the dead woman, the parcel in his arms began to cry.

"A baby?" muttered Frollo as he unwrapped the blanket to look inside. "No, a monster!" he gasped when he saw the poor, misshapen infant within.

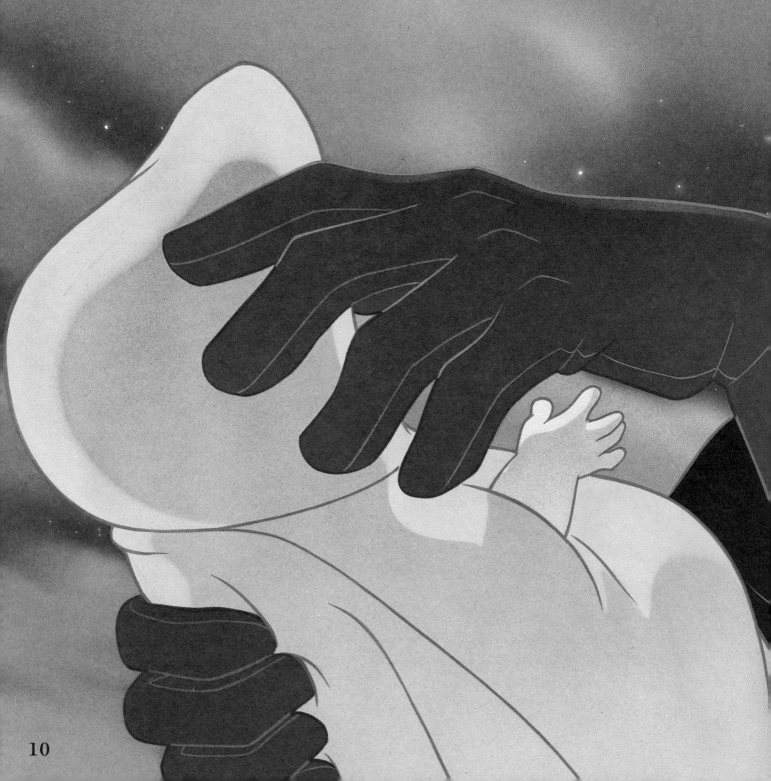

Frollo was about to drop the baby into the dark opening of a well when the voice of the Archdeacon pierced the night and stopped him. Under the watchful eyes of Notre Dame, Claude Frollo suddenly feared for the fate of his soul. When he asked the Archdeacon what he should do, the priest told him to adopt the infant and raise him as his own. Frollo agreed, but only if the child could live in the bell tower of Notre Dame.

Then Clopin posed a riddle to his spellbound audience: "Now can you guess who is the monster and who is the man?"

High above, in the bell tower of the cathedral, there lived a gentle young man who did not know of Clopin or the tale he told. Nor did the young man know anything of the world that existed below other than what he observed from his tower home. His name was Quasimodo, and he had spent every day of his twenty years in Notre Dame, where it was his task to ring its magnificent bells.

Although Quasimodo lived alone, he had three constant and faithful companions — Hugo, Victor, and Laverne. To everyone else, these creatures were merely stone gargoyles, but to the sweet-tempered Quasimodo, they were living, talking friends. Today the trio was looking forward to their annual ritual of watching the Festival of Fools with their human companion.

But Quasimodo just went inside and gazed sadly at the perfect miniature of the city he had built in his room.

Laverne followed Quasimodo and asked, "Did you ever think of going to the festival?"

"That's all I ever think about," he told her. "But I'd never fit in out there. My master, Frollo, has told me I'm not . . . normal."

But the gargoyles insisted he attend the festival until, finally, Quasimodo agreed to go.

Just as Quasimodo reached the doorway, Frollo appeared. As they went over Quasimodo's daily lessons, Quasimodo revealed that he had been thinking about going to the festival. Frollo convinced Quasimodo that he could protect the young man from the certain cruelty of the townspeople only if he stayed in the cathedral.

Down in the square, the beautiful gypsy Esmeralda played the tambourine. While her mischievous goat Djali danced to the music, passersby dropped coins into a hat. In the crowd was the handsome Phoebus, Frollo's new Captain of the Guard, who had just arrived in the city. His eyes met Esmeralda's, and for a moment they held each other's glance. But another gypsy signaled that trouble was near. Djali quickly grabbed the hat in his teeth, spilling the coins onto the ground. As Esmeralda rushed to gather the money, two soldiers approached.

Certain she had stolen the coins, the soldiers grabbed Esmeralda and snatched away the hat. Esmeralda struggled to get free, and with a little help from Djali — who butted one of the soldiers in the stomach — she finally escaped. Phoebus commanded his horse, Achilles, to sit on the other soldier, giving Esmeralda and Djali time to disappear down an alley.

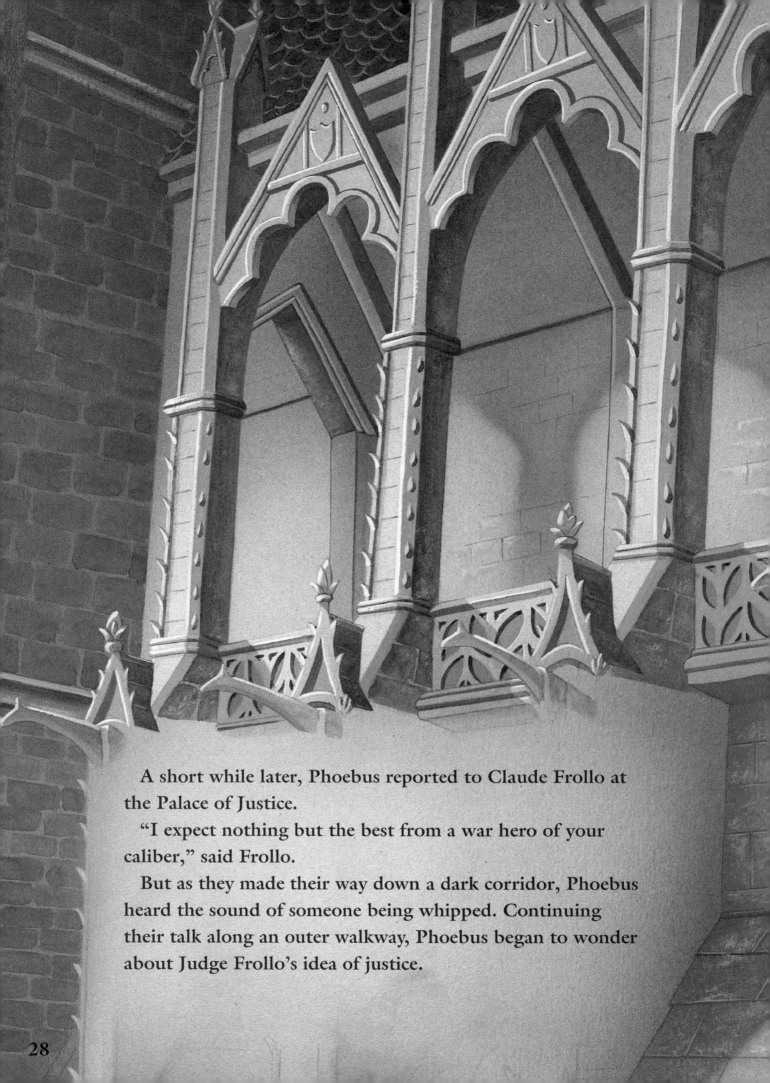

A short while later, Phoebus reported to Claude Frollo at the Palace of Justice.

"I expect nothing but the best from a war hero of your caliber," said Frollo.

But as they made their way down a dark corridor, Phoebus heard the sound of someone being whipped. Continuing their talk along an outer walkway, Phoebus began to wonder about Judge Frollo's idea of justice.

"Look, Captain — gypsies," said Frollo gravely, pointing down to the eager crowd around the dancing Esmeralda. "I believe they have a safe haven within the walls of this very city. They call it the Court of Miracles."

"And what are we going to do about it, sir?" asked Phoebus. In answer, Frollo took a stone and crushed a nest of ants he had found hidden under the railing.

Meanwhile, Quasimodo's friends, the gargoyles, had finally
convinced him to go through with his plan to attend the festival.
Disguised in a hooded robe, he climbed down the side of the
cathedral. The Topsy Turvy Day Parade was in full swing —
everywhere people were dressed in funny costumes, musicians
played, and peasants danced in the square. Although he tried to
remain out of sight, Quasimodo could not avoid being swept up in
the action.

As he searched for a place to hide, the anxious young man lost his balance and fell into Esmeralda's dressing room.

"You're not hurt, are you?" the lovely gypsy asked. She pushed his hood aside, while Quasimodo cowered, waiting for the shriek he was certain would follow.

But Esmeralda just complimented him. "Great mask!" she said.

Quasimodo roamed the square, thrilled by the festivities. Soon it was time for Esmeralda to perform. She danced her way over to Frollo on the reviewing stand. The judge could not take his eyes off the gypsy girl. Neither could Phoebus or Quasimodo. Esmeralda even winked at Quasimodo as she passed by, making him blush.

When she finished dancing, Clopin reappeared onstage to announce the crowning of the King of Fools.

As people in grotesque masks scrambled onto the platform, Esmeralda saw Quasimodo and pulled him up on stage. Esmeralda went down the line of contenders for the King of Fools, removing each one's disguise. But when she reached Quasimodo, she realized that he wasn't wearing a mask, after all!

The crowd gasped, but Clopin said, "We wanted the ugliest face in Paris. Here he is!"

Quasimodo was paraded through the streets as the ugliest King of Fools ever, but soon the crowd got out of hand, and began to throw fruit and taunt him. Frollo did nothing, even when the frightened Quasimodo was tied to the pillory and pleaded for his help.

Esmeralda came to Quasimodo's rescue, enraging Frollo, who ordered the gypsy girl arrested. In a mad chase she dodged the soldiers, and soon she and Djali slipped into the cathedral. Phoebus followed, but instead of arresting her, he told Frollo that Esmeralda had claimed sanctuary. The Archdeacon came to her side, ensuring that no harm would come to her within the cathedral's walls.

Upon his return, Quasimodo watched Esmeralda as she explored the cathedral. When he ran off to his room, she followed, wanting to apologize for what had happened at the festival.

Up in the bell tower, Esmeralda complimented Quasimodo on the miniature model of Paris he had carved. Talking to this kind person, Quasimodo began to think that what Frollo had said about the gypsies being bad might be untrue. And when Esmeralda told him he was not the monster his master said he was, Quasimodo desperately wanted to believe her.

44

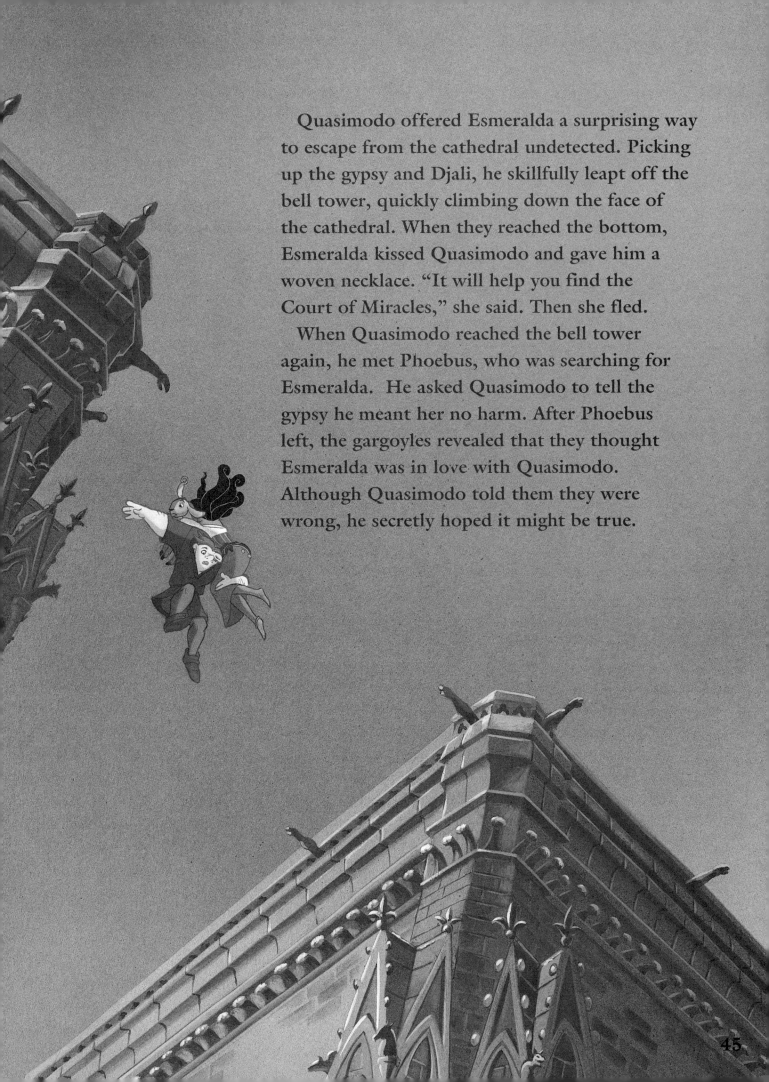

Quasimodo offered Esmeralda a surprising way to escape from the cathedral undetected. Picking up the gypsy and Djali, he skillfully leapt off the bell tower, quickly climbing down the face of the cathedral. When they reached the bottom, Esmeralda kissed Quasimodo and gave him a woven necklace. "It will help you find the Court of Miracles," she said. Then she fled.

When Quasimodo reached the bell tower again, he met Phoebus, who was searching for Esmeralda. He asked Quasimodo to tell the gypsy he meant her no harm. After Phoebus left, the gargoyles revealed that they thought Esmeralda was in love with Quasimodo. Although Quasimodo told them they were wrong, he secretly hoped it might be true.

When Frollo learned that Esmeralda had escaped from Notre Dame, he ordered his soldiers to search every building in Paris. Maddened by his unsuccessful search, Frollo even set fire to the home of a miller, certain that the family had sheltered gypsies.

At that moment, Phoebus realized how truly evil Frollo was. The brave captain entered the burning mill and rescued the family. Frollo immediately sentenced him to death. As Phoebus was about to be executed, Esmeralda frightened Frollo's horse, and Phoebus escaped.

As he fled, Phoebus was wounded by an arrow, and fell into the river. Though Frollo left him for dead, Esmeralda rescued him, then brought him to Notre Dame.

At first Quasimodo thought that Esmeralda's visit meant that she indeed had tender feelings for him. Then he realized that she had come only as a friend, wanting him to hide Phoebus. When he overheard her speaking to Phoebus, it became clear how much Esmeralda cared for the captain. Quasimodo's heart broke.

As Frollo's carriage unexpectedly pulled up outside, Esmeralda turned to Quasimodo and said, "Promise me you won't let anything happen to him."

Frollo went to Quasimodo's room and sat at the table that hid Phoebus. Frollo noticed Quasimodo was acting strangely, and became suspicious. Soon he spotted the little carved figure of Esmeralda that Quasimodo had added to his toy village. "She will torment you no longer," said the judge, setting the doll on fire and turning to leave. "I know where her hideout is . . . and tomorrow at dawn I attack with a thousand men."

As soon as Frollo left, Phoebus asked Quasimodo to help him find Esmeralda. But Quasimodo, hurt and confused, and afraid of disobeying Frollo again, refused to go with him. Sadly, Phoebus went off on his own.

Finally, thinking of his friendship with Esmeralda, Quasimodo decided to help Phoebus find the gypsy and save her from Frollo's men.

With Frollo watching, Quasimodo caught up with
Phoebus and showed him the amulet. Quasimodo explained
that it was a map of Paris, and they followed it to the
cemetery. There Quasimodo found a hidden staircase
beneath the graves, and the two descended into the darkened
tunnels. Quietly, the skeletons lying about them — who were
really gypsies in disguise — arose and began to follow
Phoebus and Quasimodo.

Suddenly they were plunged into blackness. When the lights returned, the two were surrounded.

"Well, well, well, what have we here?" said Clopin as he stepped out of the crowd. Phoebus and Quasimodo were escorted to a scaffold in the center of the amazing place, where two nooses awaited them. Clopin had them gagged, then held a make-believe puppet trial in which they were quickly found guilty of being Frollo's spies.

As Quasimodo and Phoebus were about to be hanged, Esmeralda burst through the crowd and mounted the platform. "Stop!" she shouted. "These men are our friends! This is the soldier who saved the miller's family, and Quasimodo helped me escape from the cathedral."

After Esmeralda had removed their gags, Phoebus turned to the crowd and announced, "We came to warn you — Frollo's coming!"

"You took a terrible risk coming here," Esmeralda told Phoebus. "It may not exactly show, but we're grateful."

"Don't thank me," protested Phoebus. "Thank Quasimodo. Without his help, I never would have found my way here."

"Nor would I!" cried Frollo, who had arrived triumphantly with an army of soldiers. He strode up to where Phoebus, Esmeralda, and Quasimodo stood, as frightened gypsy families tried to escape.

"He led me right to you, my dear," Frollo said, sneering at Esmeralda. "He never lets his master down."

"Then you must have tricked him!" accused Esmeralda.

Quasimodo was horrified. His friends were captured, and it was all because of him. As the soldiers led Esmeralda and Phoebus away in chains, Frollo ordered his charge to be chained up in the bell tower.

By nightfall, a platform had been built in the square. Frollo appeared, and as two guards tied Esmeralda to the stake, he announced, "The prisoner has been found guilty of the crime of witchcraft. The sentence . . . death!"

Nearby, Phoebus was imprisoned in a cage surrounded by guards. He watched, helpless, as Frollo approached Esmeralda.

In the bell tower, Quasimodo knelt motionless and defeated, while the gargoyles urged him to save his friend.

Then Frollo's voice boomed from below. "She stands before you, exposed for the monster that she is!" he proclaimed.

"No!" Quasimodo shouted as he began to tug at his chains. Quasimodo pulled with all his might, and soon the pillars that held him crumbled. He was free!

Quickly, Quasimodo swung down the wall of the cathedral and landed on the platform in the square, where he rescued Esmeralda. As soldiers rushed at him, he held them off with a beam. Then he carried Esmeralda back up the face of Notre Dame as the crowd watched in amazement.

Unharmed, Quasimodo hoisted himself onto the balcony and raised the unconscious Esmeralda above his head.

"Sanctuary!" he called. "Sanctuary! Sanctuary!"

"Seize the cathedral!" screamed Frollo, even though he had no authority over the church.

Inside the bell tower, Quasimodo placed Esmeralda on a bed of straw. He walked out onto the balcony and saw Frollo's soldiers surrounding the cathedral.

Quasimodo heaved wood and pieces of masonry over the side of the cathedral, sending soldiers fleeing in all directions. Then he picked up a beam and hurled it over the side of the balcony. It crashed onto Frollo's carriage.

Meanwhile, Phoebus had seized the guard's keys and freed himself and Clopin from the carts where they had been imprisoned.

"Citizens of Paris," Phoebus shouted, "Frollo has persecuted our people, ransacked our city . . . and now he has declared war on Notre Dame herself. Will we allow it?"

"NO!" shouted the angry crowd as Clopin and Phoebus led them toward the cathedral.

Inside Notre Dame, Quasimodo and his gargoyle friends were holding off Frollo's troops any way they could. Quasimodo was tiring; it seemed the soldiers would never stop coming. He could hear the doors of the cathedral giving way under the battering of the troops.

"It's hopeless," he muttered, resting for a moment.

Then he had an idea!

Hugo and Victor fanned the flames under the huge vat of lead Quasimodo kept in the bell tower. Quasimodo used all his strength to tip it over, and the glowing liquid flowed over the side of the wall and in front of the cathedral's doors like a red-hot curtain.

The soldiers dropped the battering ram and scattered, leaving Frollo alone in his rage.

Frollo dodged the shower of lead, and pried the cathedral door open with his sword.

Looking out from the bell tower, Quasimodo rejoiced. "We've beaten them back!" he cried. "Esmeralda, wake up! It's safe now!"

But Esmeralda continued to lie motionless.

Frollo stood in the doorway of the bell tower room, watching Quasimodo weep over Esmeralda's limp body.

As Quasimodo knelt, Frollo raised a dagger above the young man's head. But Quasimodo saw Frollo's shadow on the wall just in time, and knocked his attacker to the floor.

"All my life you have told me that the world is a dark and cruel place," said Quasimodo as he towered over Frollo. "But now I see that the only thing dark and cruel about it is you!"

Just then a voice called out softly, "Quasimodo."

It was Esmeralda! Quasimodo ran to her side and picked her up as Frollo, his sword drawn, pursued them out onto the balcony. Frollo slashed at Quasimodo as he tried to hold onto Esmeralda with one arm. Quasimodo swung around the edge of the balcony, but Frollo continued to attack, cutting Quasimodo's wrist.

Finally, Quasimodo was able to carry Esmeralda to safety. Then he climbed atop a gargoyle and faced Frollo.

After a struggle, both Quasimodo and Frollo fell from the balcony. Esmeralda grabbed Quasimodo's hand and kept him from falling further, while Frollo was able, at the last moment, to climb onto another gargoyle.

Now with Esmeralda in striking distance, Frollo raised his sword. Just then, the gargoyle under him cracked off the cathedral, and Frollo plummeted to the square below.

Esmeralda could hold onto Quasimodo no longer. She lost her grip on his hand, and he, too, began to fall. Quickly, Phoebus leaned out from below and caught their noble friend.

As the morning dawned, all the people of Paris worked to remove the traces of Frollo's rampage. When the cathedral doors opened, Esmeralda and Phoebus walked into the square, hand in hand. A moment later, at Esmeralda's beckoning, Quasimodo emerged into the sunlight. The curious crowd surrounded him, no one quite knowing what to say or do. Then a little girl walked up to Quasimodo and gently touched his face.

"Three cheers for Quasimodo!" cried Clopin.

In the bell tower high above, Hugo, Victor, and Laverne smiled as they watched the happy scene below. "Hip! Hip! Hooray!" shouted the jubilant crowd as they carried Quasimodo on their shoulders through the square. "Hip! Hip! Hooray!" they cried as they celebrated the hero of their city.